W9-ADN-540

Dedicated to the hardworking haenyeo of South Korea
— T. C.

Dedicated to the water, islands, and all of
their protectors
— J. X. S.

KOKILA
An imprint of Penguin Random House LLC, New York

Text copyright © 2020 by Tina Cho
Illustrations copyright © 2020 by Jess X. Snow

Penguin supports copyright. Copyright fuels creativity, encourages
diverse voices, promotes free speech, and creates a vibrant culture. Thank
you for buying an authorized edition of this book and for complying with
copyright laws by not reproducing, scanning, or distributing any part
of it in any form without permission. You are supporting writers and
allowing Penguin to continue to publish books for every reader.

Kokila with colophon is a registered trademark of Penguin Random House LLC.

Visit us online at penguinrandomhouse.com

Library of Congress Cataloging-in-Publication Data is available.

Printed in China | ISBN 9781984814869

10 9 8 7 6 5 4 3 2 1

Design by Jasmin Rubero | Text set in Plantin MT Infant

The art for this book was created digitally with
hand-painted textures and line work.
    With gratitude to Yuan Zheng, Zoraida Ingles, and Sean Devare
for their contributions to the making of the art in this book.

THE OCEAN CALLS

A HAENYEO MERMAID STORY

written by
TINA CHO

illustrated by
JESS X. SNOW

Kokila

Dayeon and Grandma stretched and watched the sun's first rays kiss the sea.

"The ocean is calling me today," said Grandma. "I must dive."

"I want to be a haenyeo like you," said Dayeon. "You're like a treasure-hunting mermaid."

But then Dayeon remembered the time she jumped off the big rock last summer while visiting Grandma. Water had filled her ears and nose, burned her eyes, and stung her skin. And worse, the deep ocean, where Grandma swam, was full of sharks and other scary creatures. Dayeon shivered.

"You can't grow into a mermaid if you don't finish your abalone porridge," said Grandma.

Dayeon held the shimmery blue abalone shell and rubbed her fingers over its holes. Grandma cleaned and boiled the shellfish from her catch to sell. But this porridge she had saved just for Dayeon.

As Grandma washed the dishes, she and Dayeon practiced holding their breath. One, two, three . . . fourteen, fifteen, sixteen . . .

Dayeon let the air escape in a long sigh.

Grandma squeezed Dayeon's hand.

"Don't worry. I learned to be a haenyeo from my mother. And now I will teach you."

After breakfast, Grandma put on sunscreen, a diving suit, flippers, a lead belt, and a mask.

Dayeon put on sunscreen, a suit, flippers, goggles, and a snorkel.

Grandma carried her tools to pluck treasures from the sea.
Dayeon carried hers to pluck treasures from the shore.
Together, they sang a haenyeo song.

"I eat wind instead of rice . . .
take the waves as my home."

On the sand, the haenyeo tromped, clumsy in their flippers.
But as soon as they dove—SPLASH!—they swam like mermaids.
Dayeon sat back, feeling like a beached urchin.
She wiggled her toes in the tide pool.

Grandma popped out of the water, whistling as she let out her held-in breath.

Again and again the haenyeo dove and came back up for air. The sea breeze carried the sound of their whistling.

Hoowii!

Dayeon climbed onto her lookout rock.
A shell gleamed under the water.

She jumped in to grab it. As the water circled her waist, she shuddered and gasped. That's when Grandma's voice echoed in her head. She said not to be afraid. The ocean is your home. Know the sea and find its gifts.

Dayeon looked around at the other girls giggling in the shallow water. She took a deep breath of hope and unclenched her fists.

The waves rushed around her ears, but she relaxed when she felt the soft touch of the sea anemone at her fingertips.

Maybe I could swim deeper.

After collecting ten sea gifts, Dayeon heard singing as
the orange globes of the haenyeo's nets floated closer like
a giant setting sun. Grandma and the others swam back.
Dayeon rolled round nets up the shore.
"I found pretty pebbles and shells," said Dayeon.
"Beautiful!" said Grandma. "Now, are you ready to dive with me?"

Dayeon set her bucket on a flat rock and looked at the sea. She gulped.

"What if I can't breathe? What if a shark comes? What if I can't escape?"

Grandma sang, "Can't you hear what the waves are saying? They're calling to us to come home."

Dayeon looked into Grandma's sweet eyes, swallowed her fear, and nodded.

Side by side, they walked. When Dayeon could no longer feel the ocean bottom, she locked hands with Grandma.

"Take a deep breath, calm your mind, and then we'll dive."

Down,

   down,

      Dayeon

        and Grandma dove, but . . .

Dayeon whistled as she let out her breath.
"Too quick," said Grandma. "Relax. Explore."

Dayeon swam right back up.

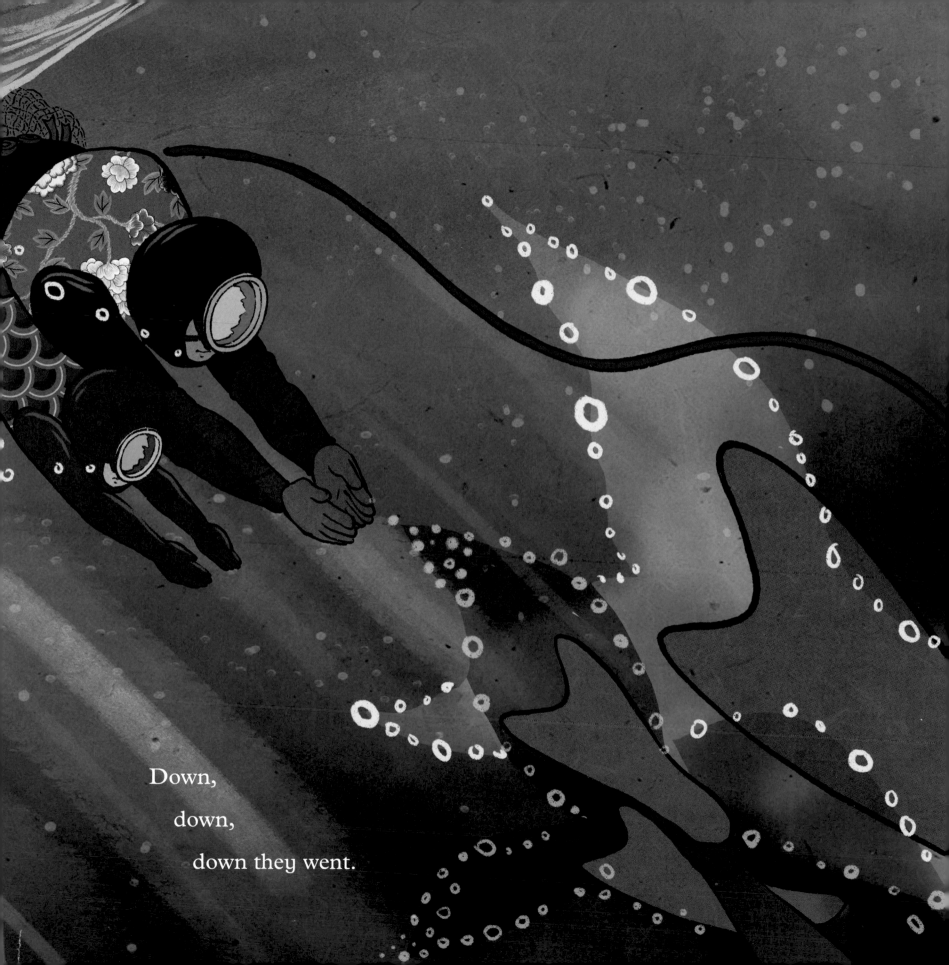

Down,

   down,

      down they went.

This time Dayeon held her breath longer. Seaweed swayed with the current. Colorful fish darted by. She pointed to a garden of sparkling treasures.

Suddenly, Grandma pulled her up, up, up.

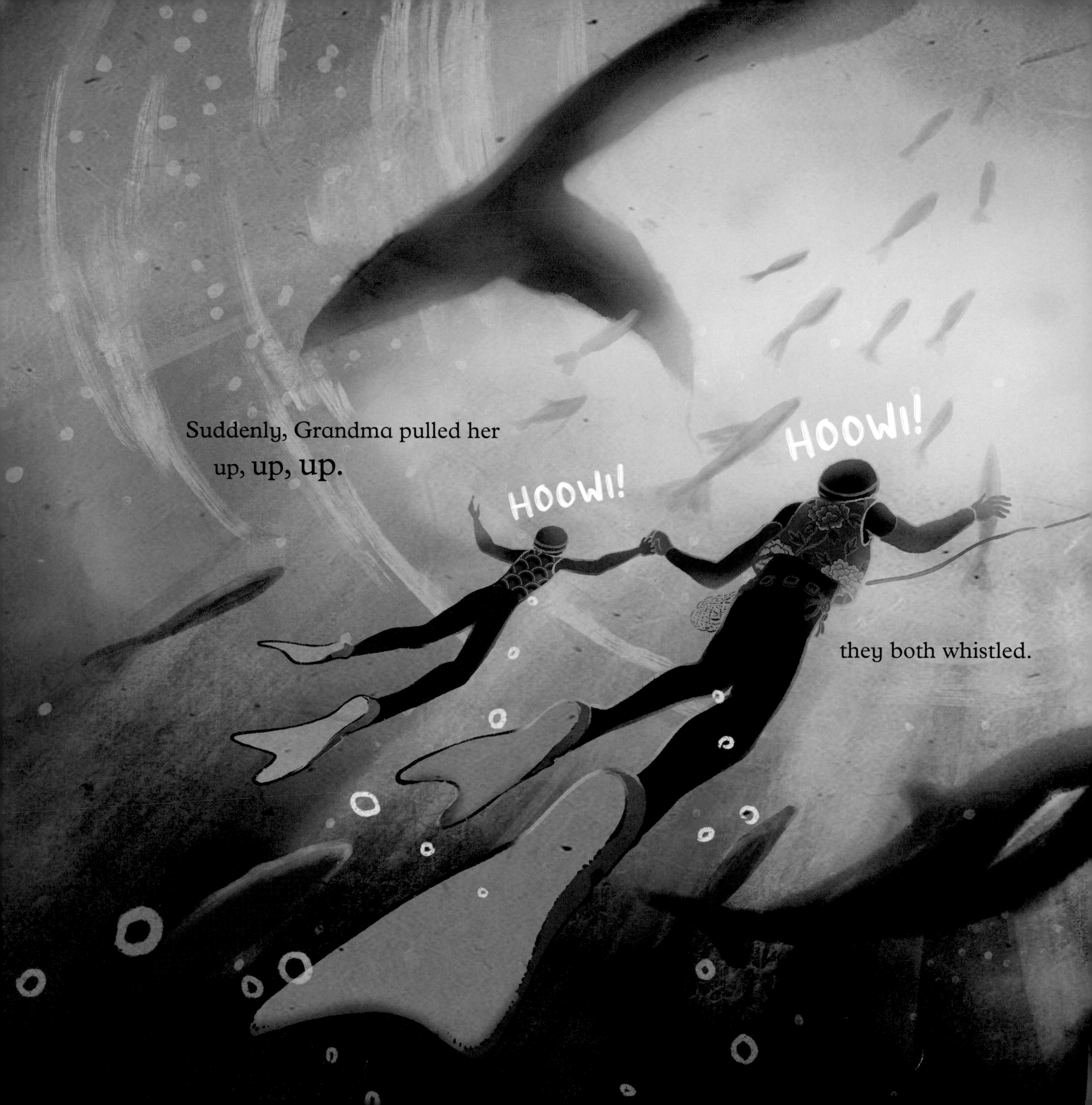

they both whistled.

"Dolphins." Grandma pointed.
"Dolphins bring hungry sharks."
Dayeon's heart beat faster. She kicked with all her might. What if they couldn't escape? Her arms felt like the lead weights in Grandma's belt.

She swam to a nearby boat. A haenyeo
waited to lift her to safety, and that's when
Dayeon remembered her wish.

Dayeon shivered in Grandma's warm embrace.
"We work together to keep each other safe. You were
brave, Dayeon. You'll be a fine haenyeo someday."
"But, Grandma, I didn't catch anything."
"Oh, but you did find treasure." Grandma opened
her hand and gave Dayeon a sparkling turban shell.

Dayeon's thumb followed the curve of the shell's spiral.
She smiled. For the first time, she felt at home in the sea.

Like a mermaid.
Like a true haenyeo.

> *"The sea makes you healthy. Just moving under the water makes you feel incredibly alive. Working like this, you feel like a mermaid."*
> **—Go Young Ja, age 79**

In March 2018, I observed firsthand the unique haenyeo tradition. Around the shores of Jeju Island in South Korea, elderly women suit up and dive in deep waters up to thirty meters. They don't use any breathing equipment and can hold their breath for up to two minutes. When they come up to exhale, they emit a whistle-like sound called sumbisori ("HOOWI!"). They sell their catch and some even cook it in restaurants. Most of the women are over fifty years old—some are in their eighties! They started diving when they were twelve to fifteen years old, and there are different levels that correspond to experience. Hagun is the beginning level and for the oldest; they dive about ten meters. Junggun is the middle level, for those plunging about fifteen meters. And sanggun is the highest—and most dangerous—level, for dives around twenty or more meters.

The word "haenyeo" is of Japanese origin, meaning "sea." The term was used during the Japanese occupation of Korea (1910–1945), and it has remained. The divers also call themselves jamnyeo or jomnyeo (Jeju dialect), which means "dive woman," and sometimes jamsu, which means "dive." To non-divers, these strong and hardworking women are fondly known as Korea's granny mermaids.

> *"We go to the Otherworld to earn money and return to the earthly world to save our kids."* **—haenyeo proverb**

The haenyeo tradition goes back centuries. History shows the giving of abalones from Jeju Island as tribute to the king during the Joseon dynasty (1392–1910). Originally, men were the divers, but in the seventeenth century, men were required to serve in the army. The king still demanded the same amount of abalone to be paid to him, so women took to the sea. Under law, women didn't have to pay taxes. They became wealthy as they sold some of their catch to Japanese buyers. The haenyeo tradition has been passed down from generation to generation.

The divers belong to a cooperative in their village where the money they make from their catch supports their families and community. Their revenue is divided according to productivity and follows the three levels of skill structure. Their association tells them who can work as well as what days and hours they can dive, and it distributes revenue. Their catch is sold through the fishery cooperative.

These working moms and grandmas do more than dive to earn a living. After spending four to five hours at sea, they head home to farm. Some don't return home until suppertime.

"I've never been ashamed of being a haenyeo. Before . . . people looked down on us. Now we're acknowledged by many people." **—Chun-hwa Ko, age 87**

Some look down on this hard way of life, where every dive is a risk of death. Many haenyeo suffer chronic back pain from wearing the almost-seventeen-pound lead belt and carrying over sixty pounds of harvest. Divers often take medicine to ward off headaches, dizziness, nausea, and vomiting. Many daughters of haenyeo have chosen to study at universities on the mainland of Korea and take other careers. As a result, there are fewer haenyeo today than there once were.

There are others who wish to preserve this tradition. The government provides the haenyeo with wet suits, medical treatment, and an annual festival to honor them. The haenyeo have been praised by international women speakers, who've called them "indigenous businesswomen and indigenous marine biologists." UNESCO inscribed the haenyeo life on the Representative List of the Intangible Cultural Heritage of Humanity in 2016. To help the tourist industry of Jeju Island, documentaries, articles, a museum, haenyeo schools, and even a tourist diving experience have shifted the perception of this profession. Haenyeo are finally receiving respect as highly skilled divers knowledgeable of marine life and aquaculture.

"We know the weather better than the weatherman. We can predict how the waves will form by the blowing of the wind." **—Kyung Ja Hong, age 70**

If the weather is good, the haenyeo dive about twenty days a month. They follow the lunar calendar, watching high and low tides. They have a map of the seabed in their minds and know how to predict the weather by watching shellfish. If shellfish cling to rocks, it means a storm is coming.

On dives, they hunt for octopuses, sea cucumbers, abalone, seaweed, turban snails, sea urchins, etc. They understand how marine life hides, when their spawning seasons are, and where they live on the ocean floor. They know not to be greedy and to take only what is needed. They are classic conservationists of marine ecology.

"We put our lives on the line together." **—Kyung Ja Hong, age 70**

These women work as a team. They follow rules such as:

- Always dive in groups.
- Check on each other to make sure everyone is okay.
- Be respectful of no-harvest seasons and no-diving zones.

A strong female community, the haenyeo share friendship, laughter, and song. Before and after dives, they used to meet at an outdoor firepit area with low stone walls called a bulteok, where they would huddle to keep warm, hang up equipment, and conduct business. Today, their bulteok resembles a locker room, and they help one another get into wet suits, take diving medication, and share life's troubles and joys. The haenyeo are driven by love for their families, nature, and one another.